Benji and Iggie
The Magic of Friendship

by Ben Kohler
Illustrations by Sandy Rummel

Edited by Rodelinde Albrecht
Illustrated by Sandy Rummel
ISBN: 978-1-64343-720-0
Library of Congress Catalog Number: 2022900436
Printed in the United States of America
First Printing: 2022
26 25 24 23 22   1 2 3 4 5

Cover and interior design by Tina Brackins

939 Seventh Street West
Saint Paul, MN 55102
(952) 829-8818
www.BeaversPondPress.com

BEAVER'S POND PRESS

     To order, visit www.ItascaBooks.com or call 1-800-901-3480 ext. 118. Reseller discounts available.

Kohler, Julie. "My 6-Year-Old Became a Storyteller This Year. It Saved Us Both." WBUR. April 16th, 2021. December 1st, 2021. https://www.wbur.org/cognoscenti/2021/04/16/pandemic-grandparent-iggie-stories-julie-kohler

A Word of Thanks

All creative works need inspiration. My inspirations are . . .

My daughter Julie, who, at age four, demanded "a real story."

My spouse Lorrie, who urged me to preserve these stories on paper.

The many friends who, over the past few years, have encouraged me to get them published.

The several librarians who helped me search the many resources I would need to access for publishing.

The authors who wrote the endless number of children's books I perused and mulled over.

My friend Sandy Rummel, who tirelessly created the illustrations.

The Beaver's Pond Press staff, who guided this neophyte children's writer through the labyrinth of the publishing process.

That voice within me that keeps generating the ideas and makes writing a joy.

And my grandson Benji, who still wants more Iggie stories.

Contents

A Warning to Kids

These stories are for grown-ups to read to kids. Kids who read them could have itsy-ditsy-oofy-doofy things happen to them. They could even get fubblewumped.

A Note to Parents

One night a long time ago, I tucked my four-year-old daughter, Julie, into bed and was tiptoeing toward the door of her dark room when I was halted by her quiet, innocent request: "Daddy, tell me a story." I had hoped to get off easily so I could settle into my evening ritual—plunk into my favorite chair, catch up on the day's news, and have quiet conversation with my wife—before retiring for the night. I fumbled in thought for several seconds, then tried: "Once upon a time, there was a bunch of kids who lived happily after." Before I could escape and close the door, her protest halted me: "That's no story! I want a real story."

So there I stood, my tuckered-out brain scrambling to find words that might release her grasp on my heart. After several seconds, some words straggled out: "Once upon a time, there was a little girl named Julie who found a young eagle that became her friend. She named him Iggie." And the Iggie stories began.

Several stories later, my wife, Lorrie, urged me to put them on paper. At first resisting, I eventually relented. But then I stashed them in a file cabinet, where they sat for years. During Julie's third or fourth year of college, I organized them into a booklet and gave them to her as a Christmas gift. As she closed her eyes and choked back tears, I did too. It was then I realized how deeply those stories had burrowed their way into both her heart and mine.

Several years later, Julie gave birth to a boy named Benji. As he grew into young boyhood, Julie and Lorrie urged me to write some Iggie stories for Benji. I resisted with all the usual excuses: "I can't think of anything to write about," "I don't have the time," "It would be too much work," and "Benji has enough books." But they reminded me how much joy those Iggie stories had brought to Julie in her childhood (and to Julie and me in our parenthood). Once again, I scrounged up some paper and put my pen to work.

 The first new Iggie story sparked Benji's imagination—and mine. Soon he wanted another, then another and another. When we got to Story #20, he informed me that he wanted a hundred Iggie stories. I gulped and started to sweat, but before long I settled in to scribble down more Iggie stories. Recently, I finished Story #84! Writing and reading these stories on FaceTime to Benji during the long months of the coronavirus pandemic and the physical separation from him became (and still is) a work of love for me. I think, for Benji too, it's a source of wonder and magic. "If these stories are working so well to create joy and magic for us," I pondered, "maybe the magic could work for others too."

All kids love stories, and parents enjoy engaging with kids in the stories they love to hear. The Iggie stories in this collection could be read as written, or they could serve as starters for adults who are creating stories for little ones. Any particulars of a story could be changed to fit a certain child: insert your child's name instead of Benji's, select parks and buildings from your neighborhood for the settings, insert the names of your child's friends, select their favorite foods—it's easy to do. Most importantly, don't forget to occasionally stop and ask your storytelling partner "And then what happened?" Don't be surprised if your child starts becoming an excellent storyteller helper. These stories will become a part of your child's magical world. My hope is that these Benji and Iggie sto- ries will help children (and adults) unlock their imagination and explode into the magic that exists in sharing and telling a story.

Benji Makes a Friend

Once upon a time, not so very long ago, there was a young boy named Benji who liked to go on long walks with his grandpa, Poppy. One day when Benji had no one to play with, he asked Poppy to take him for a walk into the Soapstone Forest nearby. Poppy, who liked the outdoors very much, said, "That sounds like a good idea. Let's go!" So they left their house and started walking down Connecticut Avenue to the Soapstone Forest.

It was a beautiful day. The sun was shining and warming the spring air. A gentle breeze tickled and rustled the wild grasses and trees. Benji held Poppy's hand, as there were many paths that twisted and turned, and if you weren't careful, you could get all mixed up and lost. That could be scary. While they walked, they listened to the birds and crickets. They even heard bullfrogs croak as they passed ponds and lakes. And they talked, oh, did they ever talk! They talked about all the things they saw—ants and caterpillars, butterflies and bees; wondering do they have brothers and sisters? Do they sleep in their very own beds? What do they eat? Do they talk? And what is it like to fly high up in the sky like the little eagle Benji noticed flying over the nearby trees?

Well, Poppy tried to answer all of Benji's questions, and overall did a pretty good job, considering how hard they were. As they came to a bend in the path, the eagle that had been gliding in the air currents high above suddenly dove, swooping down at them to land in the path ahead of them so close you could almost touch it. They were very startled, and Benji's grip on Poppy's hand tightened even more.

Poppy said, "Benji, we should start walking back, because we don't want to frighten the little eagle."

But as they were turning, Benji stopped and said, "Wait! I don't think the eagle is scared. It looks friendly—maybe it wants to be friends."

Benji took two timid steps toward the eagle and held out his hand. The eagle hopped toward Benji, flew up, and landed on his shoulder.

Benji cried out, "See, Poppy? He's a gentle eagle, and he really does want me for a friend."

"Well, I'll be fubblewumped!" Poppy replied. "I've never seen anything like this before in my entire life."

The eagle then took off from Benji's shoulder, flying up to circle their heads once before swooping so close to Poppy's head he had to duck. *Whomp*! Poppy fell backward into the tall grass, landing right on his behind.

"Watch out!" Poppy shouted. "That bird is up to big mischief; we'd better get out of here fast!"

But Benji laughed and said, "Oh, Poppy! I don't think the eagle will hurt you. He played a trick on you, and you sure look funny sitting there in the long grass." The eagle landed on Benji's shoulder and waited for Poppy to get up and brush himself off.

"I think this eagle is young, like me," Benji said.

"I think you're right; grown-up eagles are much bigger," Poppy replied.

"Let's give my little eagle friend a name."

Poppy rubbed his chin and thought really hard. "Hmm . . . how about Clyde?"

"No, no, no!" Benji exclaimed.

"Well then, let's try Harold or Waldo," said Poppy.

Benji interrupted him, "No, never; those are awful names for a little eagle!" "Well, I can't think of any more names," Poppy said. "I'm fubble fubblewumped."

Benji thought and thought, and finally he shouted, "Iggie! I'll call him Iggie." The moment he said "Iggie," the little eagle flapped his wings, flew up and landed on Benji's shoulder again, looking very happy.

So they walked through the woods with Iggie on Benji's shoulder until Iggie flew up, circled around them a few times, and headed back to his nest in the Soapstone Forest. Benji smiled and waved goodbye to Iggie.

"Can we come back here again so I can see my new friend?" Benji begged, pulling on Poppy's arm. "Please, Poppy, please?"

Poppy smiled. "Sure we can, but only if that darn Iggie doesn't land me on my behind again with a *whomp*."

They both laughed as they turned to walk back home. Benji was thinking about how easy it is to make friends when you are friendly. Benji could hardly wait to tell his Mommy and his grandma—Nanny—about his new friend, Iggie the eagle. And that's the story of how Benji made a very special friend that day.

Benji Finds His Finger Friends

One Saturday morning when Benji woke up from a good night's sleep, he jumped out of bed and got dressed as fast as he could. He had so many fun things to do that day with his friends—go to the pool, ride his bike, see all the animals at the zoo, sit in his yard while they blew bubbles and shot balloon rockets, go to the playground, and walk to the ice cream shop for a special treat. But when he looked outside he saw it was raining.

"When will it stop raining so I can have fun outside?" he asked his Mommy.

"Oh, Benji, it's supposed to rain all day," she told him. "I think you will have to find things to do inside today."

Suddenly, all the happiness Benji had felt about a fun day playing with friends outside was washed away by the rain. He felt disappointed and sad. He was mad at that darn rain for ruining his day. He didn't want to be miserable all day, but he didn't know what to do about it.

He thought about throwing toys around his room, but that wouldn't make the rain go away. He was too big to cry. And if he crawled under his bed to wait for the rain to stop—well, he would get tired of trying to hide from the rain.

"What can I do?" he asked his Mommy. "I *don't* want to read books all day. I'm tired of drawing and painting pictures, and I *don't* want to clean my room."

Mommy sat down beside Benji. "Why don't you get out your finger puppets?" she asked him. "Remember how you talk to them, and they always like talking with you? Or maybe you should get your magic wand and wish for your friend Iggie to fly here. Eagles can fly through the rain, and your magic can bring him right into your room."

At first Benji thought that wouldn't work at all, because he couldn't remember where his little finger friends were. But his Mommy suggested he look for one or two and they could help him look for the others. Benji thought it wouldn't hurt to look for one or two; and there was nothing better to do with it raining all day anyway. And—his magic wand—yes! He could do lots of magic with Iggie and his little friends. His Mommy always had good ideas.

He started pushing through his box of LEGO blocks—and there was Flossy! She looked up and said, "Thank you, Benji. I was worried that you would never want to play with me again." He put Flossy on one of his fingers and she pointed right to his chair. Sure enough, they looked under the chair and found Gwumple, whose eyes were big like he was just waiting to be found.

Benji put Gwumple on his finger and he pointed to Benji's closet. When Benji opened the door he found Crunchy chewing on a pretzel. Benji had named the puppet Crunchy because he was always chewing on something crunchy. Now he had three little friends on three fingers. They all pointed to his bed. When Benji lifted up his pillow he found Foofie, and they all cheered.

"Benji," Foofie called out, "I like sleeping in your bed, but please don't leave me under your pillow for so long; it gets too hot for me!" Now the only two left to find were Pinky and Grundoon. Benji and his friends hurried to look under his dresser, where they found Pinky.

"Benji, thank you for finding me," Pinky shouted. "I was getting lonely under there." He now had five of his finger friends on his five fingers. But then Benji heard a muffled cry from the far corner of his room.

"Hey, don't forget about me! I don't want to be stuck under your pile of stinky socks. Get me out of here!" It was then that Benji remembered he was always forgetting about Grundoon. Benji lifted up his pile of socks

"Hey, that's better!" Grundoon called. "You try spending the night under some stinky socks. It isn't fun." And all the little finger friends cheered because they always had the most fun when they all got to do things with Benji. Benji turned to Grundoon.

"I have six finger friends but only five fingers on one hand," he explained. "You are special, so you get to have your own hand. And you can always pick which finger you want to be on. From now on your name will be 'Don't Forget Grundoon' because that will help me remember never to forget you."

"I like my new name," Don't Forget Grundoon nodded and told him, "And I won't be miserable anymore about being left behind."

Already Benji's day indoors was getting better.

"Benji, what can we do that's different and fun, so no one complains about not being able to go outside?" Foofie asked.

Benji smiled. "Wait here. I'll get my magic wand and ask my friend Iggie the eagle to visit. He will help us have super-duper fun!"

As Benji waved his magic wand, he told his finger friends to close their eyes, count to twenty, and say the magic words *uffa huffa muffa wuffa, up, up and away!* In an instant, SWOOF! Iggie flew into Benji's room and landed on his head. All his finger friends laughed because who ever saw an eagle sitting on someone's head?

"Iggie likes to play tricks," Benji said with a chuckle. "I just got fubblewumped.Now, close your eyes and say the magic words again for a fun surprise."

Everyone said the magic words *uffa huffa muffa wuffa, up, up and away*, and presto chango— Gwumple, Foofie, Flossy, Crunchy, and Pinky flew off Benji's fingers and started following Iggie around the room!

"Hey! Don't forget about me!" yelled Don't Forget Grundoon. Benji lifted him off his finger and Don't Forget Grundoon started flying faster than all the others, right behind Iggie. Then they all sat in a circle around Iggie and Benji and dreamed up a few good ideas for fun inside the house on this rainy day. They played hide-and-seek and follow-the-leader, did loop-de-loops, and had flying races. They were so busy all day that before they knew it, it was late afternoon and Benji's Mommy was asking who would like an ice cream treat.

"I do, I do," they all yelled. Except Don't Forget Grundoon, who shouted, "Hey, Don't forget about me." They flew to the dining room table to eat their own big dish of ice cream.

Then it was time for Iggie to fly back to his nest in the Soapstone Forest and for the finger friends to return to the little basket where they could rest. When Benji looked out the window, he saw that it had stopped raining. He knew then that tomorrow would be a sunny day and he would be able to go outside. But he was happy he had tried Mommy's suggestion to do some magic and make a rainy day fun.

Benji Has a Hot Dog Dream

One night when Benji was getting ready for bed, he did all the fun things—changed into his jammies by himself, read two of his favorite books with his Mommy, and then jumped into bed and snuggled up under his blanket. But Benji couldn't fall sleep right away. He kept thinking about the last delicious hot dog he had eaten. He wished he could have one right then.

"Mommy, I can't sleep, because I want a hot dog," Benji called out. "But I know I can't have one because it's time to sleep."

Mommy came into the room and sat on the edge of Benji's bed, listening as he told her his problem.

"I don't want to stay awake and be unhappy all night because I can't have a hot dog," Benji explained. "I know I'm too big to cry about it. What can I do?"

"Benji, do you remember how good ideas come to you when you stay calm and don't yell or scream?" his Mommy asked softly. "And do you remember how you and Iggie can do magic? Why don't you get your magic wand, close your eyes, take deep breaths, and wish for Iggie to fly here to be with you tonight? And maybe—just maybe—Iggie can bring a little magic to help you dream about a hot dog."

Benji liked that idea. When he and Iggie help each other, he gets lots of ideas for all kinds of fun magic they can do. And if Iggie were with him in his bed, he's sure he would fall asleep faster. Benji thanked his Mommy for the good idea. Then he closed his eyes, said the magic words—*uffa huffa muffa wuffa*—and wished with all his might for Iggie to come and be with him so he could dream about eating a delicious hot dog.

Well, the magic started working. Benji closed his eyes and began to feel less unhappy. Before long he heard the faint *fllp-fllp-fllp* of Iggie's wings as he flew into the room. But Benji was already dreaming. Iggie landed on Benji's pillow and gently waved his wing over Benji's head. Benji smiled in his sleep because this meant Iggie was going to help his dream come true. Iggie, being an eagle, didn't talk like people talk. But with the special magic Benji used, Iggie was able to whisper into Benji's ear. Iggie told him to keep breathing softly and imagine a hot dog floating into his room and resting close enough on his pillow that he could smell it and touch it. And sure enough: Benji dreamed of a hot dog, a dream so real his mouth started to water. He could almost bite into that hot dog, chew it, and taste it. Benji was dreaming about the biggest and best hot dog he would ever eat.

But the dream only got better. Before long, Benji's little finger friends—Gwumple, Foofie, Flossy, Crunchy, Pinky, and Don't Forget Grundoon showed up in his dream. They climbed up into Benji's bed from their little basket on the floor and sat on his blanket. Don't Forget Grundoon—who always complained the loudest—spoke first.

"Hey, Benji, what about us little people? We like hot dogs too. Are you going to dream about us going hungry? That's making me cry—*wah wah boo hoo sob sob slobber slobber.*"

Benji's little finger friends laughed because Don't Forget Grundoon's laughing and crying always sounded funny.

"Benji, remember it's good to share things with your friends," Pinky said. So Benji and Iggie waved the magic wand and brought hot dogs to everyone. Hot dogs began floating around the room.

"Holy catfish, dogfish, sunfish, monster fish!" all the finger friends shouted. "Look at all the hot dogs." Everyone reached out, grabbed one, and started eating a hot dog.

"Look," Pinky exclaimed. "I got a pink hot dog."

Foofie's hot dog came with mustard. Flossy got her wish for one with pickle relish and ketchup. They ate so fast that murmurings of *yum yum yum mmm yummy* was the only sound that filled the room.

Of course Crunchy's hot dog had pretzels that made a *crunch crunch crunch* sound whenever he bit into it. And then there was the foot-long hot dog for Don't Forget Grundoon. Gwumple had to help him eat it because it was much too big for him to finish on his own. Benji took two big bites of his hot dog, garnished with his favorite toppings, mustard and ketchup. His hot dog even had a surprise of a jelly bean hidden in the bun—a treat for later.

Benji was about to take a big bite of his hot dog when he noticed a very sad look on Iggie's face. You see, Iggie had never eaten a hot dog and didn't know what to do. He was just as hungry as everyone else, and it was no fun looking on as everyone else was enjoying scrumptious food.

"Here, Iggie," Benji said, "take a bite of my hot dog. Don't be afraid; hot dogs are good food." Iggie took a bite, then another bite, and then *another* bite. Pretty soon he had eaten most of Benji's hot dog, and he wanted more. Benji laughed and told Iggie they needed to do more magic to bring more hot dogs. Iggie flapped his wings. Benji told all his little friends to help by saying the magic words—*uffa huffa muffa wuffa, up, up and away!* And—*POOF!*—more and more hot dogs instantly appeared.

Ha ha ho ho hee haw ho ho ho, Don't Forget Grundoon shouted as he stopped crying and started laughing. That made everyone else laugh too. Iggie was super happy because Benji had helped him try a new kind of food that he liked. Altogether they ate sixteen hot dogs, including two foot-long hot dogs that Don't Forget Grundoon and Gwumple shared.

As the dream ended, Benji drifted into a deep sleep. When he woke up the next morning he ran to tell his Mommy about his magic dream about not just one hot dog, but enough hot dogs for all his friends. Benji thanked his Mommy for the great idea to do this super-duper wooper magic with Iggie. He couldn't wait to tell all his friends at school about the best dream he ever had.

And that's the story of the time Benji, Iggie, Gwumple, Foofie, Flossy, Pinky, Crunchy, and Don't Forgot Grundoon had a magic hot dog party in Benji's dream.

The Mystery of the Missing Cupcakes

B enji liked to play a game with his Mommy called the cupcake game, where they took turns looking at big pictures of cupcakes—more than forty of them. Of course Benji had his favorite cupcake, his second favorite cupcake, and even more favorite cupcakes. He told Mommy that he wished his favorite cupcakes were real so he could eat them with all their good frosting.

"Benji, why don't you get your magic wand?" his Mommy said. "If you wish with all your might, maybe your cupcakes will become real."

Benji liked that idea very much, so he ran to get his magic wand. As Benji waved his magic wand over a picture of the cupcakes, he said the magic words *"uffa huffa muffa wuffa*, magic, make my cupcakes real!… And bring Iggie here because I want to show him how to eat cupcakes."

And, *SWOOF!* Iggie landed and sat next to Benji, and all the cupcakes became real—even Mommy's favorites. As he gazed at the platter of cupcakes, just waiting to be eaten, Benji knew he was in cupcake heaven.

But Iggie looked puzzled. He had never seen cupcakes before and didn't know they could be eaten. So Benji dipped his finger into one with green and yellow frosting and brought it to Iggie's beak. Iggie nibbled at the frosting and then swallowed a little before taking a small bite of the cupcake. Iggie flapped his wings to show that he liked the cupcake. But it was getting late.

"Benji," his Mommy said, "It's past your bedtime. Let's put the cupcakes on the table and get ready for bed. Iggie can sleep with you tonight. Tomorrow you can do more magic so Iggie and all your little finger friends—Gwumple, Foofie, Flossy, Crunchy, Pinky, and Don't Forget Grundoon—can have a cupcake party."

Benji was disappointed that he couldn't eat cupcakes right then. But he remembered what Pinky always said: sometimes we all have to wait for the things we like most. So Benji helped his Mommy carry the cupcakes to the table and he and Iggie went to bed, with Iggie snuggling up next to him. That night, Benji had the best dream ever about eating cupcakes.

The Mystery of the Missing Cupcakes

The next morning Benji woke up and ran to the table, but two of his favorite cupcakes were missing! Uh-oh! Something bad had happened during the night. He knew he would need help to solve the mystery of the missing cupcakes. He ran back to his bed and nudged Iggie to wake him. Benji told Iggie about the missing cupcakes and they went to work right away looking for clues. Benji found some cupcake crumbs on the floor of the living room.

"I found a clue," Benji shouted to Iggie. "Keep looking; maybe we can find more."

Iggie flew into the hallway and flapped his wings to let Benji know he had found more crumbs. Benji ran to look.

"Iggie, these crumbs are close to my room. Let's look in there." Both of them crouched down on the floor and looked carefully. Sure enough—they found a trail of crumbs that led under Benji's bed. Iggie flapped his wings.

"Iggie, I think we are getting close to solving this mystery. We can't give up now."

They both peered under the bed. There, in the far corner against the wall, they spotted Gwumple, Flossy, Foofie, Crunchy, Pinky, and Don't Forget Grundoon, faces covered with frosting and cupcake crumbs all around them.

"What the hoozy woozy!" Benji shouted. "Iggie, I think we solved the mystery of the missing cup-

23

cakes. We found the cupcake thieves, and they are my little friends!"

Benji asked his friends why on earth they would steal the cupcakes. Foofie explained that it was Crunchy's idea. After Benji and Iggie went to sleep, they would place two cupcakes near Benji's bed just in case he and Iggie woke up hungry during the night. But while they waited under the bed, Don't Forget Grundoon's tummy started to grumble.

"Psst! Hey, everyone, I'm hungry!" Don't Forget Grundoon whispered loudly. "And if Benji and Iggie don't wake up, these cupcakes might get stale just sitting here. Let's eat just a little bit to make sure they are still okay to eat."

The finger friends looked around at each other and each gave a nod, agreeing to take a little bite. But the cupcakes tasted so good they took another bite, and another, and before long they were covered in frosting and stepping on cupcake crumbs.

"Benji and Iggie," Pinky chimed in, "Eating the cupcakes was a bad idea. We were only trying to bring a treat for you and Iggie. We're sorry."

"Yeah, I'm sad and so sorry that I'm going to cry—*wah wah boo hoo sob sob slobber slobber*," whined Don't Forget Grundoon.

Well, it was so funny listening to Don't Forget Grundoon cry that they all started to laugh.

Benji and Iggie looked at each other and

smiled. They knew friends didn't mean to do something bad. And it was nice that they wanted to do something good for them—have two cupcakes close by in case they got hungry during the night.

"It's okay," Benji said. "We have lots of other cupcakes. Let's go tell Mommy about how we solved the mystery of the missing cupcakes."

In the dining room, Mommy listened carefully to Benji's story.

"Thank goodness nothing really bad happened," Mommy said. "Let's all have a cupcake!"

They all picked out a favorite cupcake and talked about how something bad like missing cupcakes could turn out to be something very small that didn't hurt anyone at all. Of course Iggie ate a cupcake, too, because Benji had taught him how to eat a new food. And because Benji had waved his magic wand to make the cupcakes real, they all had a super fun cupcake party. And that's the story of the mystery of the missing cupcakes.

Benji and Iggie Ride the Carousel

One day when Benji's Nanny and Poppy were visiting, Benji asked if they could go to the Washington D.C. zoo. "And can I ride the carousel?" Benji asked. They thought that sounded like a fun idea. So they left Benji's home and started walking down Connecticut Avenue to the bus stop. Suddenly they heard a swooping noise and saw something flying around their heads.

"Oh, my goodness! What was that?" Nanny exclaimed.

"Holy catfish, dogfish, sunfish, monster fish! We're being attacked by something from outer space," Poppy shouted.

Benji just laughed and said, "Don't worry; it's Iggie, and he wants to go to the zoo with us." Iggie landed on Poppy's head and wouldn't leave.

"Oh, no! That darn Iggie," Poppy grumbled. "Now everyone will think I'm some itsy ditzy oofy doofy goofball sitting on the bus and walking through the zoo with an eagle on my head." Benji smiled because he knew this was just one of the funny tricks Iggie liked to play.

So they got on the Metro bus and rode to the zoo. People just giggled as they looked at Poppy with Iggie sitting on his head. When they arrived at the zoo and started walking, Benji named all the animals he wanted to see—the elephants, tigers, peacocks, ducks that went *quack quack*, birds that went *tweet tweet tweet*, and of course the panda bears. So they walked to all the areas where these animals lived. Suddenly, lots of kids shouted to their mommies and daddies: "Look! there's an eagle sitting on that man's head." People smiled and thought this was the funniest thing they had ever seen at the zoo.

Poppy smiled back and explained, "That's Benji's friend Iggie. He likes to play funny tricks like this." Poppy wondered if Iggie was going to do more of his oofy doofy tricks when they got to the carousel. Nanny bought tickets for herself, Poppy, and Benji. The woman at the ticket counter said Iggie could ride, too, but would have to ride with Benji on his horse. Benji and Iggie jumped onto a horse that had Benji's favorite colors, brown and white.

The carousel started moving slowly. The organ music got louder and the drum went *boom boom*. A zillion lights flashed in a hundred mirrors. Benji and Iggie laughed as they rode up and down and round and round on the carousel. The people watching were amazed to see a real eagle riding the carousel with Benji. As the horses galloped faster and faster, Iggie flew up and away from Benji.

"Uh-oh, Benji," Poppy shouted, "It looks like your Iggie friend is flying away. Maybe you will never see him again." But Benji wasn't worried because he had whispered to Iggie that he should do some magic. Iggie flew back to the carousel, landed on Benji's horse, and flapped his wings.

And that's when the magic happened. Their horse started running away from the carousel with Benji and Iggie.

"Oh, dear," Nanny screamed. "There goes Iggie taking Benji away. Maybe we'll never see them again!"

"Holy catfish, dogfish, sunfish, monster fish!" Poppy shouted. "Iggie is doing something more than an oofy doofy trick; he's kidnapping Benji! Quick! Stop the carousel! Call the police! Call the firefighters! Call an ambulance! They could fall and get hurt!"

But as Benji and Iggie were flying on their horse up and over the trees and all around the zoo, Benji was happy because Iggie was helping their horse fly. Their magic made them safe.

"Look up in the sky! That horse, eagle, and boy are flying!" everyone at the zoo shouted as they looked up at Benji and Iggie. All the kids at the zoo wished they could fly like that too.

Then Iggie and Benji and their carousel horse came down from the sky and landed back on the carousel. The carousel slowed down and the ride ended. The organ and drum music stopped.

"Well, I was real scared and got fubblewumped," Poppy muttered while shaking his head. "And I guess everybody at the zoo today got fubblewumped."

Benji and Iggie came running back to Nanny and Poppy. Benji told them the carousel was so much fun they should hop on horses again and ride into the sky.

"I'm not doing that," Poppy said. "Maybe your and Iggie's magic would stop working when I'm up above the trees and I would fall into the den of the grizzly bears. And I would have to run fast so the bears wouldn't bite me on my behind."

Benji laughed because he knew that the magic always worked, and nobody would get hurt. By then it was time to leave the zoo and ride the Metro bus back to Benji's home—with Iggie sitting on Poppy's head, of course. Poppy played along, smiling as people giggled over how funny he looked with Iggie on his head. As they got off the bus, the driver told Benji she hoped Iggie would ride on her bus again.

Seeing Iggie sit on Poppy's head had

made the bus ride fun for her and all the passengers on the bus.

And that's the story of the time Benji and Iggie got a magic ride on the Washington D.C. zoo carousel.

Benji and Iggie Rescue Poppy

One day when Benji's Poppy and Nanny were visiting, Benji asked if they could go outside so Iggie could do some magic with them. Nanny said she couldn't go because she was busy helping his Mommy in the kitchen, but Poppy jumped up out of his chair with excitement.

"Sure, Benji! I'll go and I would like you and Iggie to do your magic so I can fly. But I don't want Iggie to make me go *WHOMP!* on my behind like when we met him in the forest."

"You won't go *WHOMP!* if you say the magic words, Poppy," Benji explained. "When we get outside, say *uffa huffa muffa wuffa*."

"*Umfwa humfwa mumfwa plumfwa*—whatever. Okay, Benji. I said those funny words. Now make me fly."

But Benji thought, "Uh-oh! Poppy wasn't listening. He said the words wrong and that could bring big trouble."

They looked up into the big tree where Iggie was waiting for them. Iggie flew down and landed on Poppy's head.

"Oh, no!" Poppy grumbled. "I can't fly with Iggie sitting on my head. People will think I'm some itsy ditsy oofy doofy goofball who wears an eagle for my hat."

Benji laughed, knowing they were about to play a fun trick on Poppy. Iggie started flapping his wings and Benji started waving his arms to get ready to start flying.

"Come on, Poppy, start waving your arms and say the magic words. And be careful to say them the right way this time," Benji instructed.

Poppy wondered why he had to say those funny words again but decided he would just go along with it to make Benji happy.

"Umfwum mumfwum fwumfwum flumflum, up, up and away," He shouted.

Sure enough, Poppy lifted up from the ground and started flying with Benji and Iggie.

Benji cringed, and whispered to Iggie, "Poppy said the magic words wrong again. I'm afraid something bad is going to happen to him."

They flew in circles over the yard, all the way up to the kitchen windows, and waved to

Mommy and Nanny, who smiled and waved back. Then Poppy started flying really fast.

"Poppy, be careful," Benji shouted after him. "If you go too fast, you could get into trouble."

But Poppy didn't listen; and he started doing circles, upsy-dupsy somersaults and loop-de-loops. Then something really bad happened. He flew right into the big tree and got stuck upside down in the branches. The harder he tried to get loose, the more stuck he became.

He yelled, "Benji, tell Iggie to do his magic and get me out of this tree."

Iggie shook his head and whispered to Benji that his magic wouldn't work, because Poppy did dumb things—like saying the magic words wrong, flying too fast, and doing all those loop-de-loops. Benji told Poppy that magic wouldn't solve his problem.

"What am I going to do?" Poppy asked. "I can't stay here forever. I can't sleep here tonight; I don't have my pajamas. And I won't get to eat supper. I am fubblewumped; worse yet—I'm fubble fubble-wumped!"

But Iggie and Benji knew how to fix Poppy's problem. They flew away north over Connecticut Avenue. Poppy began to really worry, thinking he would never get unstuck and would have to live forever in a tree. He looked down and saw all kinds of people stopping to look up at him. They laughed because he looked so funny being stuck upside down with his right leg wrapped around his neck.

"Holy catfish, dogfish, sunfish, monster fish! There's a grandpa upside down in a tree," one boy shouted. He asked Benji's Poppy how he got stuck in the tree. Poppy was afraid to try and explain that he flew there. He thought people would think he was some kind of itsy ditsy oofy doofy goofball making up a crazy story about getting stuck in a tree.

Benji and Iggie flew to the fire station nearby and told the firefighters that Poppy needed their help. Soon a siren sounded, and the big fire truck came racing down Connecticut Avenue. Benji and Iggie were riding in the back seat and wearing their fire helmets. They showed the firefighters where to find Poppy up high in the treetop. The firefighters rushed out from the truck, took out their long ladder, and climbed up to rescue Poppy. When they got back down on the ground, they asked him what he was doing that he got stuck in this big tree. Again Poppy was afraid if he told them he had been flying and said the magic words wrong they would think he was some itsy ditsy oofy doofy goofball so he just said: "Um, well, I uh, er—well, I got lost." They looked at one another, scratched their heads, and just said: "Well, next time you go outside, don't get lost." They got into the fire truck and went back to the station. Benji and Iggie just laughed, because this was the funniest thing that had ever happened when they were with Poppy. And Benji couldn't wait to tell Mommy and Nanny about the funny way Poppy got stuck in a tree.

And that's the story of the time Benji and Iggie—and the firefighters—rescued Poppy while he was flying.

Benji and Friends
Ride in the Fire Truck

O ne of Benji's favorite things to do was to watch the fire trucks whiz by, sirens blaring and lights flashing, on their way to put out fires. One day when he was walking with his Poppy, they were near the fire station in his neighborhood.

"Poppy, can we go to the fire station?" Benji asked.

He wished that someday he could get really close to a fire truck and maybe even ride in one. At school he had learned that firefighters were very friendly. They liked to show kids their fire trucks and teach them about all the equipment they used to put out fires. As they got to the big doorway of the fire station, Benji stopped.

"Wait, Poppy. I want to invite my friend Iggie. I know he would like to see a real fire truck."

Of course Benji knew just what to do to make Iggie appear. He pulled out his magic wand, closed his eyes, waved the wand and said the magic words—*uffa huffa muffa wuffa, up, up and away!* And—*SWOOF!*—Iggie came swooping into the fire station and landed on Benji's shoulder.

Well, Benji did such a good job saying his magic words that a most unusual thing happened. All Benji's little finger friends—Gwumple, Foofie, Flossy, Crunchy, Pinky, and Don't Forget Grundoon—appeared with Iggie.

"Thank you for doing special magic so we could be here," Foofie said to Benji. "We're so small we can't go anywhere on our own. And we've always wanted to see a real fire truck, not just one that you read about in bedtime books."

Benji was happy that his little friends could be with him at the fire station. Before Benji could ask the firefighters if they would show them everything about putting out fires, the fire chief noticed them standing outside.

"Holy catfish, dogfish, sunfish, monster fish!" she shouted to the firefighters. "Everyone get out here quick! We have a young boy and an eagle and a bunch of real little people visiting our fire station. This is most unusual. We'd better do a super job showing them everything about how we put out fires."

Then, just as the firefighters started showing them the fire hoses and their fireproof coats and fire helmets, the fire alarm went off—*ding ding ding ding ding!*

"Quick, everyone, get into the fire truck," the fire chief shouted. "Benji, get your eagle friend and the little people into the back seat with the firefighters. We can't leave you here."

Poppy said he would stay at the fire station so the fire truck wouldn't be too crowded.

One firefighter ran up to the truck, shouting, "Here are the firefighter helmets you'll need to wear when we go to the fire."

The helmets fit Benji and Iggie, but they were so big that you couldn't see the little people under them. But that was okay because they were happy just riding in a real fire truck.

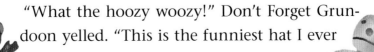

"What the hoozy woozy!" Don't Forget Grundoon yelled. "This is the funniest hat I ever

wore. I can't see anything. And I feel like laughing—
ha ha ho ho hee hee haw haw ho." Everybody laughed
at the funny sounds he made whenever he laughed.

The fire truck roared down Connecticut Avenue
with its siren going all the time—*whoo whoo whoo.*
Cars slowed and stopped to make room for the fire
truck to zoom past with its siren blaring loudly and
its lights blinking red, white, and blue. When they
arrived at DuPont Circle, everyone jumped out of
the fire truck.

The firefighters said, "Benji, take all your friends
and look for places where there is fire; then tell us so
we can bring our hoses and spray water on the fires."

Iggie went one way while Benji and his little
friends went the other. They all came back to the
firefighter and pointed to where they had found the
fires burning. The firefighters were then able to put
out the fires and bring their equipment back to the
fire truck. As they rode back to the fire station, all
the firefighters thanked Benji, Iggie, and his friends
for helping them put out the fire. Without their help,
the entire house might have burned to the ground.

When they got back to the fire station, Benji and
Iggie jumped out of the fire truck. Benji told Poppy all about their ride down Connecticut Avenue
to the fire near DuPont Circle, including how Iggie
had flown around to show the firefighters where to
aim their water hoses and how he and his little

friends had run around and helped the firefighters put the fire out quickly.

"Holy catfish, dogfish, sunfish, monster fish, Benji," Poppy said. "That's really good! And the firefighters wouldn't have been able to fight the fire if you and your little friends hadn't been there."

Just then the firefighters walked over. "Benji, we want to make you, Iggie, and all your little friends special firefighter helpers." They gave each of them a medal they could wear and keep at home in a special place. Benji smiled and Iggie flapped his wings and then flew around the fire station until it was time for Benji to walk back home with Poppy and his little people friends. It was also time for Iggie to fly back to his nest in the Soapstone Forest. As Iggie flew up and away, everyone waved goodbye to him. And that's the story of the time Benji, Iggie, and all his little friends rode in the fire truck and helped the firefighters put out a fire.

A Special Birthday Party

As Benji's sixth birthday got closer, he told his Mommy that he wanted to invite Iggie to his birthday party. Iggie was Benji's best friend, and they liked doing fun things together—like going on bike rides, riding in a fire truck and helping firefighters put out fires, playing tricks on grown-ups, and having playtime together. Mommy said he could invite Iggie and all his school friends to his birthday party.

Benji was really excited that Iggie could come. He talked to Iggie and together they planned all the surprise magic they would show his friends. On the day of Benji's birthday party, everybody gathered outside in his backyard. Then Iggie came swooping down—*SWOOF!*—from the big tree and landed on the ground in front of everyone. All the kids cheered because they liked Iggie. When it was time for the games to start, Benji told everyone to close their eyes and count to twenty. They closed their eyes really tight and started counting—one, two, three, and all the way to twenty—and then said the magic words— *uffa huffa muffa wuffa, up, up and away!* When they opened their eyes, they saw Iggie sitting on Benji's head. "Benji, you look funny with Iggie sitting on your head," everyone shouted and laughed. Benji laughed too. "I just got fubblewumped," he said.

Then Benji told everyone to close their eyes again and get ready for a fun trick. When they opened their eyes, Iggie was sitting on Ellie's head. Then he jumped onto Frankie's head. Everyone laughed again. This trick went on and on until Iggie had sat on everyone's head. They all tried to say they got fubblewumped, but it was a word they had never heard, and it was pretty hard to say. Benji said it so fast it came out sounding like *fwumblefwumpf, fwub-bleewuff, or flufflefwumb.* The funniest way they said it was *fumwumbfflffwuffmumpf.*

They played a few more games and then it was time for birthday cupcakes. Benji's Mommy brought a plate of cupcakes covered with chocolate, strawberry, lemon, and blueberry frostings. Everyone picked their favorite cupcake.

"Now Iggie will do his next trick," Benji announced. "Close your eyes, count to twenty, and put your hands behind your backs."

This wasn't as easy as it sounded because everyone wanted to start eating their cupcakes right away. While their eyes were closed, Iggie flew up, used his beak to pick up a cupcake, and placed it on Benji's head. Then he delivered a cupcake to every kid at the party, each time placing it on their head. When they opened their eyes they all laughed; it looked so funny to see everyone with a cupcake on their head.

"Now you have to take turns eating the cupcake on the head of the kid next to you with your hands behind your back," Benji said.

At first they all just looked at each other and wondered how they would eat a cupcake without using their hands. But when one kid stuck her nose in the next kid's cupcake frosting, everyone wanted to give the game a try. It wasn't easy because they were giggling so hard and getting frosting smeared all over their faces. After a while, though, they all managed to eat the cupcakes. Their faces were covered with red, green, blue, orange, and yellow frosting. They talked about whose frosting face looked the funniest.

"Now it's time for Iggie to do super birthday magic with us," Benji said. "Close your eyes tight, wish with all your might for the magic to happen, and count to twenty. Oh, and don't forget to say the magic words—*uffa huffa muffa wuffa, up, up and away!*"

This time they all said the magic words right. As they opened their eyes, Iggie flapped his wings and lifted up from the ground.

"Now, wave your arms up and down really fast," Benji told them.

All the kids did, and they lifted up from the ground.

"It's magic; I'm flying; I'm flying!" So they all followed Iggie as he led them on a flying parade around and around in circles and then high up above the treetops. People walking nearby were amazed at all the kids flying above them.

"Holy catfish, dogfish, sunfish, monster fish!" the bystanders shouted. "There are kids and an eagle flying everywhere. If they get stuck in trees, they will miss their supper! And kids can't sleep in trees; they don't have their jammies. We'll have to call the firefighters to climb up their long ladders into the trees and bring those kids down."

But they didn't need to do that. Slowly Iggie and all the kids flew down and landed on the grass. Now for the best part: it was time for all the kids to lick the frosting off their faces. Only they couldn't lick it off their own faces, so they licked the frosting off the face of the kid next to them. That was the craziest way to get your face washed. And it took forever because it's hard to lick frosting off someone's face when you can't stop laughing. But when all was said and done, they did have very clean faces.

Then it was time to go home. They all thanked Benji for making this the best birthday party they had ever been to. As they were leaving they tried to remember the magic words and that funny fubblewump word. They tried really hard to say it, but they got everything mixed up. It came out like *umfwa fumbfwa wuffamubwum fufflemuffa up, up and away.* Well, at least they got the last magic words right.

Just trying to say those funny words had them laughing all the way home. They couldn't wait to tell their mommies and daddies about flying around the treetops and the crazy cupcake game.

And that's the story of the time Iggie and Benji did magic at his birthday party.

The Foot Fairy
Visits Benji

One day as Benji was moving his tongue along his teeth, he found a tooth that was loose and almost ready to fall out. His mommy had told him that after a tooth fell out, he could put it under his pillow and the tooth fairy would bring him a gift. But—oops—Benji's tooth fell out the next morning when he was eating his breakfast . . . and he swallowed it. But that didn't matter. The tooth fairy always knows when a tooth falls out, and she makes sure to place a gift under the kid's pillow. Sure enough, that night the tooth fairy brought Benji a set of colored pencils.

The next day Benji told his Poppy and Nanny on FaceTime about the tooth fairy.

"I heard a long time ago that there is also a foot fairy who will bring you a gift if you put your foot under your pillow when you go to bed," Poppy told

Benji. "I don't know if that's true, but it makes me wonder if that could really happen."

Benji thought that sounded funny but that it wouldn't hurt to try to find out. So that night as he sat on his bed he tucked both feet under his pillow. He wanted to stay awake to see if the foot fairy would come. And to make sure the foot fairy is real he waved his magic wand and said the magic words: "*Uffa huffa muffa wuffa*, Foot Fairy, Foot Fairy, come here tonight."

Knowing his magic always worked, Benji felt ready to go to sleep. His Mommy said it would be too hard to sleep sitting up with his feet under his pillow. But Benji wouldn't move his feet, and it was getting very late.

"Benji, you don't have to sit up all night with your feet under your pillow for the foot fairy to come," Mommy explained. "He knows that kids need to lie down and rest their head on their pillow to get a good night's sleep. I'll get you an extra pillow to cover your feet." So Benji lay down and snuggled under his blanket with his head on his soft pillow and his feet under the extra pillow. He tried to stay awake so he could see the foot fairy come into his room. But he was so tired that he fell asleep and had a happy dream about the foot fairy flying into his room and very quietly placing a gift under his pillow.

The next morning when Benji woke up, he lifted his pillow and there was the gift—a new pair of purple and yellow socks. He held them tight in his hand, jumped out of bed, and ran to Mommy's room to show her his special gift from the foot fairy. Later that day he and Mommy were talking on FaceTime with Poppy and Nanny. Benji showed them his socks from the foot fairy and told then all about how it happened. Poppy wondered if he put his foot under his pillow that night, would the foot fairy bring him a gift? Benji wasn't so sure that the foot fairy brought gifts for grandpas. But Poppy wanted to find out for himself. So that night he put not just one foot but both feet under his pillow and kept them there all night. He wanted to make sure the foot fairy would visit and leave him a special gift. Nanny thought that was a funny way to sleep.

The next morning when Poppy woke up he lifted the pillow and found his special gift from the foot fairy—a stinky old sock. When he told Benji about it later that day on FaceTime, Benji said that the foot fairy played a trick on him.

"What the hoozy woozy! I got a stinky old sock!" Poppy said, scratching his head. He wondered what he should do with his funny gift. "Benji, I don't need an extra sock and I don't want a stinky old sock; would you like it? I could send it to you in the mail."

"I don't want a stinky old sock. Don't send it to me," Benji laughed. So Poppy was stuck with the stinky old sock.

Then Benji looked out the window.

"Mommy, Mommy, look!" Benji shouted. "There's an eagle flying around just outside and it's carrying a sock in his talons. It's not a really big eagle. I think—I think it must be my friend Iggie!" Benji told Poppy all about it. "What?" Poppy asked. "Iggie was flying outside your window and carrying a sock? I think maybe you are just making this up. And maybe this whole thing about the foot fairy is just pretend. Maybe last night I walked in my sleep and got a stinky old sock that was way back in a corner of my closet."

Benji got very serious and said, "Poppy, the foot fairy has to be real. How else would I get a new pair of yellow and green socks? And how would that stinky old sock get under your pillow? You would never do that yourself. It has to be that the foot fairy put it there. He played a trick on you. And I think Iggie is the foot fairy, and he can do magic just like I can. How else would he know where I live? He's an eagle. They can fly anywhere. Iggie flew all the way to your house in Minnesota and must have put that stinky old sock under your pillow. The sock he is carrying must be the other stinky old sock. Should I ask Iggie to take it to you?" "No! I don't want more stinky old socks," Poppy shouted. He scratched his head again and mumbled, "Well, I'll be fubblewumped. I suppose you are right—there really is a foot fairy and it's Iggie the eagle. I suppose now I have to worry if that darn Iggie is going to play more tricks on me."Benji laughed. "I think so, Poppy, because Iggie can do magic and he likes to play tricks."

Benji couldn't wait to tell all his friends about the magic he could do with his magic wand, about how Iggie liked playing fun tricks, and how funny it was to know that his Poppy got fubblewumped sitting on his bed wondering what to do with the stinky old sock he was holding.

And that's the story of how Iggie the foot fairy visited Benji and played a trick on Poppy.

Benji Helps Iggie Get Well

Benji was getting ready to go outside and play when all of his little finger friends—Gwumple, Flossy, Foofie, Crunchy, Pinky, and Don't Forget Grundoon—told him they wanted to go along too. They really wanted to see some of the magic that he and Iggie could do.

So they went outside to the big tree where Iggie was always waiting for Benji. But Iggie wasn't there. Of course Don't Forget Grundoon was the first to complain. "Hey! Where's Iggie?" Don't Forget Grundoon whined. "We want to play with him. I'm so unhappy I could cry—*wah wah boo hoo sob sob slobber slobber.*"

"Is Iggie mad at us? Did he just forget that we are his friends?" Foofie asked.

"Iggie'd better get here because Don't Forget Grundoon will drive us crazy with his sob sob slobber slobber crying all day," Crunchy said.

"Don't worry," Benji told them. "Iggie would never forget to come play with his friends. Let's wait. Maybe Iggie had to help clean his nest before he left."

So they waited and waited, and then they waited some more.

Finally Pinky shouted, "Look; I see Iggie coming."

"Yippy dippy woopy doo!" they all cheered.

But Iggie was flying very slowly, and when he arrived he didn't land on anybody's shoulder like he usually did. Instead he landed on the ground and just sat there, looking tired and sad.

Iggie wanted to play with all Benji's friends. But every time he tried to play tag or hide-and-seek he would stop and just sit on the ground. They all knew something wasn't right with Iggie and started to worry. Flossy and Gwumple got really close to Iggie and asked him why he looked so unhappy. Iggie could only whisper that he was lonely and hadn't been able to play with them for a long time. He was afraid that maybe they didn't like him anymore. He didn't feel like doing anything and couldn't sleep. He was feeling terrible.

Mommy and Nanny came out of the house to watch everyone play. They knew right away that Iggie was sick.

"Maybe we need to drive Iggie to the eagle doctor," Benji said.

"No," both Mommy and Nanny replied. "That would take too long. We don't know what else to do. But maybe if Iggie could get back to his eagle nest and get some quiet rest, his mommy eagle can care for him. Maybe then he'll begin to feel better."

"Wait here," Benji said. "Take care of Iggie and I'll get my magic wand and do magic."

He ran into the house, dug out his box of toys, found his magic wand, and ran back outside. They all cheered when they saw Benji with his magic wand.

"Everyone, close your eyes, take deep breaths, count to twenty, and say the magic words with me— *uffa huffa muffa wuffa, up, up and away!*" Benji said.

As soon as everyone said the magic words, they all lifted up from the ground. Everyone except Iggie, that is, because he wasn't feeling well. Benji picked up Iggie and held him really snug in his arms.

"Okay, everyone; I'll carry Iggie. Let's fly to his nest in the Soapstone Forest." Iggie opened his eyes a little and nodded, as if to tell them that was what he wanted.

Benji's friends started flying high above the trees, following Benji, who held Iggie really tight so he wouldn't fall.

"Hey, this is cool!" Don't Forget Grundoon shouted. "We're like doctors and nurses helping Iggie get better. And I'm done crying."

When they got to Iggie's nest, his mommy and daddy eagle were happy to see Iggie come home. They'd been worried when Iggie flew out to play when he hadn't looked very healthy. Benji gently put Iggie in his nest and Iggie fell asleep right away. Benji told all his friends they should leave so Iggie could sleep without being disturbed. And Iggie's mommy and daddy eagle thanked everyone for bringing Iggie home.

Benji and his friends all flew back to Benji's yard, where they played lots of games; but it wasn't as much fun without Iggie. Soon they all went home, promising to come back tomorrow morning. Everyone hoped Iggie would be feeling better by then.

In the morning, they gathered under the big tree—but there was no Iggie. They were sad and worried about their friend.

But then Gwumple shouted, "Hot diggity dog diggity doo diggity doo! Look above the trees. It's Iggie; he's flying fast and is doing loop-de-loops up and down. I think he's feeling better now."

"Hip hip hooray! Ipsy dipsy doopy do!" Everyone cheered.

Iggie started dancing and jumping around; then he hopped on top of the heads of all the little people. He wanted to spread a little of the magic that Benji and he had made to everyone. It worked; soon they all lifted up and were flying around the yard.

Iggie led them in a parade over the trees and down the street to the ice cream shop. When they got there, Iggie landed on the shoulder of the ice cream lady and whispered something into her ear. She smiled and made ice cream cones for everyone. This bit of magic was the way Iggie said thank you to Benji and his little friends for helping him when he was sick.

After eating their ice cream cones, everyone flew back to Benji's yard. They played kickball, hide-and-seek, and a new game called catch-me-while-I-fly, which turned out to be the best new game they had ever learned. Everyone was extra happy because Iggie was no longer feeling sick. In fact, it was the most fun they had ever had.

"Benji, that was so nice of you to have us help take Iggie home when he was sick. That made us all happy," Pinky said.

And that's the story of when Benji and his friends did magic to help Iggie get well.

The Easter Bunny Visits Benji

On the day before the Easter Bunny was supposed to come, Benji was busy coloring Easter eggs with his Mommy and wondering what good candy and other things the Easter Bunny would bring him this year. He also wondered what his little friends Gwumple, Foofie, Flossy, Crunchy, Pinky, and Don't Forget Grundoon were hoping for. The only way to find out, of course, was to ask them. So he dug into his toy box and brought them to the table.

One by one, he asked each of his little friends what they wanted. Gwumple wanted chocolate-covered Cheerios; Foofie wanted lemon drops; Flossie wanted cotton candy; Crunchy wanted candy-covered potato chips that would go *crunch crunch* when he chewed on them. Pinky wanted any kind of candy as long as it was colored pink, just like her. Don't

Forget Grundoon, who grumbled if things weren't just how he liked, thought really hard about what he wanted.

"Hey! I want candy-covered snowballs with spaghetti and milk toast. And if the Easter Bunny doesn't bring me that I'll be so sad I'll cry all day every day until next Easter time," he blurted out.

All the little people laughed because when Don't Forget Grundoon cried—*wah wah boo hoo sob sob slobber slobber*—it made them laugh. And listening to him cry every day for a whole year would be the most itsy ditsy oofy doofy goofball thing they would ever have to listen to.

As Benji was getting ready for the Easter Bunny's visit that night, he remembered that he wanted Iggie to be with him for the Easter treats. So he said the magic words—*uffa huffa muffa wuffa, up, up and away! And—SWOOF!*—Iggie flew into Benji's room within a minute. When Benji told Iggie what would happen that night, Iggie flapped his wings and started flying around the room; getting candy sounded like fun even though he didn't know what candy was, because eagles eat fish and other little animals to grow big and strong. Benji placed some carrots on the kitchen table for the Easter Bunny. Bunnies like carrots and the Easter Bunny would be very hungry that night after working hard to deliver candy to kids.

Before bedtime, Benji and his friends listened as Mommy told them bunny stories. Then they all snuggled under the blankets with Benji to dream about the sweet treats and toys the Easter Bunny would bring. But then, just when everyone was starting to fall asleep, Don't Forget Grundoon piped up.

"Hey, Benji," he shouted, "I got an idea. You and Iggie could do some magic to make us wake up when the Easter Bunny comes. We can invite her to stay for an all-night Easter Bunny candy party. And that will make me so happy that I won't have to cry until next Easter."

Benji and Iggie talked quietly and decided it would be fun to try. They would do some super-duper wooper special magic so the Easter Bunny could stay for the candy party and still have time to deliver candy to kids everywhere.

"Close your eyes, count to twenty, and say the magic words—*uffa huffa muffa wuffa*, come on, Easter Bunny! Wake us up when you come and stay for an Easter candy party," Benji told them.

They all repeated the magic words and then fell into a deep sleep, dreaming and hoping that the magic would work. Then, in the middle of the night, Benji woke up.

"Shhh," he whispered to everyone. "I hear something in the kitchen. I think I can hear the sound of candy being dropped into our Easter baskets. And now I hear some crunchy sounds; she might be eating the carrots I put on the table for her. Let's all get out of bed real quiet-like and tiptoe into the kitchen."

As they all peered around the corner into the kitchen they couldn't believe their eyes. Sure enough, the Easter Bunny was there, eating her carrots.

"Surprise! Surprise, Easter Bunny!" they all yelled. "We did magic so we would wake up to see. Will you please stay for an all-night Easter candy party? Please, please, stay and make this the best Easter ever!"

Well, the Easter Bunny couldn't say no, because Benji, Iggie, and all his little friends were so friendly and nice to invite her to a candy party. She was so surprised her ears wiggled and all she could say was, "Well, I'll be fubblewumped." Everybody laughed because nobody ever heard of a bunny being fub-blewumped. So the Easter Bunny stayed while they all shared the good candy she had brought.

"This is the first time I was ever invited to an Easter party," the Easter Bunny told them. "And it makes me super happy. Thank you for putting carrots on the kitchen table for me. I was really getting hungry after bringing candy treats to lots of kids."

"Easter Bunny, we all agreed that it would be a nice thing to have a party for you," Pinky said. "Benji reminded us that because you are so good to kids it would be a nice act of kindness to treat you and let you rest from all your hard work." The Easter Bunny smiled and told them this was the nicest thing anybody had ever done for her. They all enjoyed their candy treats and got ready to go back to bed. But first they waved goodbye to the Easter Bunny as she hopped away to deliver more candy to other kids everywhere.

And that's the story of the Easter Bunny's visit to Benji and Iggie and Gwumple and Foofie and Flossy and Crunchy and Pinky and Don't Forget Grundoon on that very special Easter.

The Mystery of the Missing Halloween Candy

One Halloween there was a big mystery in Benji's house. After he had gone trick-or-treating around the neighborhood, he placed all his Halloween candy in a big dish on the kitchen table. The morning after Halloween, Benji went to the kitchen to get a piece of candy. But—uh-oh! There was no candy in his candy dish. Benji was very sad and angry that all his candy had disappeared. He asked Mommy if she knew what happened. Mommy told him she had no idea how that could have happened. But then she thought about it a bit more.

"Benji, I think that during the night when you were sleeping I heard some noise coming from the kitchen," Mommy explained. "I was half asleep and didn't think to get up and find out what the noise was. But I wonder if somehow someone got into the kitchen and took your candy. Now you have a problem. Your candy is gone. What do you think you should do?"

Benji thought really hard. "Mommy, I think I should wave my magic wand and ask Iggie to come here and help solve this mystery."

So that's what Benji did. He closed his eyes, scrunched up his face, counted to twenty, waved his magic wand, and said the magic words—*uffa huffa muffa wuffa, up, up and away!* And—*SWOOF!*—Iggie appeared in their kitchen, standing right next to the empty candy dish. In only one minute, Iggie had flown from his nest in the Soapstone Forest all the way to Benji's house. Iggie stood quietly on the kitchen table with a puzzled look on his face. He was clearly wondering why Benji had made this emergency magic call for him. Iggie had been very busy that morning trying to solve the mystery of his lost little eagle neighbor. He was tired after a long search for the little eagle and the trip to take her back to her nest.

"There was a noise while I was sleeping, and this morning when I woke up all my Halloween candy was gone," Benji explained.

Iggie, who had never talked because he was an eagle, could talk now because of the special emergency magic that Benji made.

"Hmm," Iggie said. "I think we have to look for clues. There was some noise. That's a clue. There must have been somebody who snuck in here, made the noise, and probably took the candy."

"Let's you and I go searching in different places for more clues," Benji suggested. "Maybe we'll catch the candy thief and get my candy back."

Benji started searching in the living room and close to his bedroom. Iggie hopped slowly into the hallway, looking into every corner.

"Iggie, here's a candy wrapper by the door to my room," Benji shouted.

Iggie flew fast to Benji's side. The two hurried into Benji's room and started looking for more clues.

"Iggie, here's another candy wrapper near my bed."

"Aha, Benji. This is a good clue. I think we are getting close to solving this mystery. The candy thief has to be nearby."

Benji looked under his bed. "Iggie, I found the candy thief. But it's not just one thief—it's six thieves, and they are my little finger friends—Gwumple, Foofie, Flossy, Crunchy, Pinky, and Don't Forget Grundoon."

They looked up at Benji and Iggie as they sat next to the big pile of Benji's candy. Of course it was Don't Forget Grundoon who spoke first.

"Holy catfish, dogfish, sunfish, monster fish," Don't Forget Grundoon shouted. "It's Benji and Iggie."

"Yay! Yah! Whoopy doopy do!" They all cheered.

Benji asked them why they were cheering after they'd been caught in the act of stealing his Halloween candy.

"Benji, we didn't steal your candy," Foofie explained. "After you went to bed we started worrying about stories we had heard on the news that there was a candy thief in the neighborhood. We decided it would be good to protect your candy. And carrying all that candy was hard work because we are so small. So, we carried all the candy and hid it under your bed. We didn't sleep all night because we were on the lookout for candy thieves. We didn't want them to sneak into the house to steal all your candy."

"Yes, Benji," Pinky added. "We all talked about being afraid that your candy might get stolen. We decided protecting your candy was the best thing we could do. But after staying awake all night, we got hungry and thought you wouldn't be mad if we each had a little candy. We hope you aren't upset that we took some of your candy."

Benji was so happy to learn about the good thing his little finger friends had done for him.

"Oh, thank you. When I first saw my empty candy dish, I was sad and angry," Benji explained. "But now I know how much you all care about me. You stayed up all night to help me. And I'm glad you ate some candy. Anybody staying up all night would get hungry. You are the best friends in the whole world."

Iggie, who had been listening to the little people explain how the mystery happened, hopped around and jumped with joy. Benji decided it was time for some super-duper magic. He told everyone to say the magic words—*uffa huffa muffa wuffa, up, up and away!* When they did, everyone was able to take off and fly around Benji's room. Benji's candy flew with them.

"It's time for a Halloween mystery solving party," Benji shouted. So Benji, Gwumple, Foofie, Flossy, Crunchy, Pinky, and Don't Forget Grundoon ate candy treats as they flew around Benji's room. Even Iggie got a candy treat.

"This is the best Halloween I've ever had!" Benji exclaimed.

And that's the story of how Benji and Iggie solved the mystery of the missing Halloween candy.

The Ticklebug Sneaks into Benji's Sleeping Bag

Benji's eagle friend, Iggie, was one of his best friends, but he had other close friends too, including his little finger puppet friends Gwumple, Flossy, Foofie, Crunchy, Pinky, and Don't Forget Grundoon. And that wasn't all. Benji had another special friend—the Ticklebug. Benji always had fun with the Ticklebug, who liked to tickle people, hide, then come back and tickle everyone some more.

Not long ago, Mommy bought Benji a sleeping bag that he liked very much. It was pink—one of his favorite colors. Benji loved to snuggle down into the sleeping bag and eat snacks. One night Benji was all ready for bed—he had jumped into his jammies, picked out two of his favorite books for his Mommy to read, and had his nighttime snack—when he thought it would be fun to have Iggie come and sleep with him in his sleeping bag. So he grabbed his magic wand, closed his eyes, scrunched up his face, and wished and wished for Iggie to come and be with him. And, sure enough—*SWOOF!*—within a minute Iggie flew into Benji's room and settled close to Benji on his pink sleeping bag.

But as he and Iggie got ready to start eating their snack, a loud shout filled the room.

"Hey, Benji," yelled Don't Forget Grundoon, "What about us little people? We like sleeping in a sleeping bag too."

"I'm sorry, Don't Forget Grundoon, Gwumple, Flossy, Foofie, Crunchy, and Pinky," Benji replied. "I got so excited about my new pink sleeping bag I forgot to call you over. Come on! Crawl into my bag and have a snack with Iggie and me."

So the little people did just that. After they all talked, finished their snack, and listened to Mommy read from Benji's favorite books, Pinky started squirming and laughing—*hee hee haw haw hee ho.*

"Uh-oh!" Benji squealed. "Somehow the Ticklebug got into my sleeping bag. He hides and then comes to tickle people and makes them giggle. I'll catch the Ticklebug and put him under my pillow where he can go to sleep."

So Benji started looking everywhere in the sleeping bag. But as he fumbled around inside the bag he started giggling; all the little people also started giggling really loud—*ho ho ha ha hee hee hoo hoo haw haw ho.* The Ticklebug was everywhere and Benji couldn't catch it. Well, it was the funniest thing ever, with everyone giggling. Iggie was squirming because he couldn't sleep with everyone giggling and jumping around. Benji had to stop looking for the Ticklebug because he was giggling so hard. He didn't know what to do to stop the Ticklebug from tickling everyone. Then he had an idea. He reached out near his sleeping bag, grabbed his magic wand and waved it, wishing for the Ticklebug to go hide so they could stop giggling and eat their snack. It worked. Everyone stopped giggling and laughed about the Ticklebug's goofy trick.

But then Benji saw that Iggie was looking sad—and confused. He wasn't getting tickled. In fact, he had no idea what it was like to get tickled. And he was the only one in the sleeping bag not having fun. Poor Iggie didn't know if he should laugh or cry or fly away. It was no good to have Iggie unhappy while everyone else was having such a happy time. So Benji waved his magic wand again, told everyone to say the magic words with him—*"Uffa huffa muffa wuffa*, Ticklebug, Ticklebug, make Iggie laugh." And the Ticklebug did just that. Iggie flapped his wings and started giggling eagle giggles. Then the Ticklebug played a trick. He jumped around, tickling Benji and Gwumple and Flossy and Foofie and Crunchy and Pinky and Don't Forget Grundoon extra fast. They all started laughing and squirming and crawling over one another as they tried to get away from the Ticklebug. Iggie was flying around inside the sleeping bag and bumping into everyone. That made the tickling and squirming even funnier. Mommy came running into Benji's room wondering what all the giggling and squirming was about.

"Holy catfish, dogfish, sunfish, monster fish!" She shouted. "What kind of sleeping bag did I get? It keeps jumping around and making so much giggle noise that Benji won't be able to sleep tonight. Benji, are you okay?"

Benji peeked out from the sleeping bag and told Mommy that they were all having fun with the Ticklebug—Iggie and all his little friends who came to be with him all night in his sleeping bag. So then Mommy knew what all the hullabaloo was about.

She shook her head and said, "Well, I'll be fubblewumped. Benji, you and your magic wand can do amazing magic."

Just then Benji found the Ticklebug and gently placed it under his pillow. The Ticklebug didn't mind this at all because he was tired from all the tickling and ready for a rest. Benji, Iggie, and all Benji's little friends were getting tired too. They all snuggled into Benji's pink sleeping bag and settled down for a good night's sleep.

And that's the story of how the Ticklebug snuck into Benji's sleeping bag and helped him and all his friends have a tickle good time.

Benji and Iggie
Make a Snowman

One of Benji's favorite things to do was visit Nanny and Poppy in Minnesota. He and his Mommy would fly in an airplane, which was so much fun. Of course he always asked Iggie to fly to Minnesota too. Iggie couldn't ride in the airplane, but Benji could use his magic to help Iggie fly alongside the airplane all the way to Minnesota. Benji enjoyed looking out the airplane window and watching Iggie wave to him as they flew high above the clouds. Benji was glad he had brought his little friends along—Gwumple, Foofie, Flossy, Crunchy, Pinky, and Don't Forget Grundoon. They also liked looking out the window and waving to Iggie as he flew as fast as the airplane.

At Nanny and Poppy's house in Minnesota, they found so many things to do. Hide-and-seek was always fun because the little people were so small they could find super small places to hide. And Benji knew the best places to hide—in closets, behind doors, and around corners everywhere.

It was winter in Minnesota, so one afternoon Poppy had the idea to go play in the snow.

"Benji, should we go outside and make a snowman?" Poppy asked.

"Yes, but I want Iggie to help us," Benji replied.

"Hmm—hum-humff!" Poppy grumbled. "I've never heard of an eagle making a snowman. Maybe Iggie should stay inside."

But Benji was persistent. "Poppy, Iggie can do magic; he can do everything!"

"Well, okay, let's give it a try. But tell Iggie I don't want any of his itsy ditsy oofy doofy tricks like getting me stuck in a big snowdrift."

Benji told Poppy not to worry because Iggie always made sure any tricks he played would be fun. So Benji and Poppy put on their winter coats, mittens, and boots and trudged out to the backyard with Iggie flying behind them. As Poppy and Benji started packing snow in their hands and rolling the snowballs in the wet snow, Iggie landed on Poppy's head.

"What the hoozy woozy!" Poppy shouted. "Iggie is supposed to help make a snowman, not take a nap while sitting on my head." Benji laughed; it was pretty funny to see an eagle sitting on someone's head while they were making a snowman. Iggie flew off Poppy's head and started flapping his wings in the snow next to the big snowball that Benji and Poppy were rolling.

"Look, Poppy!" Benji said. "Iggie is helping us pack the snow into a big snowball for the first part of the snowman."

"Well, I'll be fubblewumped," Poppy replied. "How did Iggie learn how to do that?"

Benji just smiled. He knew it was because of their magic. And then Iggie, Benji, and Poppy started another snowball, rolling it in the wet snow until it was just a little smaller than the first one. Poppy lifted it and placed it on top of the bigger ball of snow. They made a third snowball, a little smaller than the second one. Poppy placed it on top as the snowman's head.

"Well, we're making progress," Poppy said. "But what should we do to make the snowman look real?"

"Poppy, the snowman needs eyes, a nose, and a mouth. And he needs arms and a cap, so he looks real."

"You're right, Benji. But where are we going to get all that stuff?"

Just then Iggie flew up and around the backyard then over the house.

"What the hoozy woozy!" Poppy shouted. "Right when we need more help to make the snowman look real, Iggie flies away." Poppy was getting angry. "What kind of a friend goes away when you need help? Maybe you should send Iggie back to Washington, D.C."

"Poppy, don't be grumpy," Benji said, laughing. "Remember, Iggie can do magic; he'll figure out a way to make our snowman real. Say the magic words."

"Let's see, *umpff fwumppf mumpfwuff*!" Poppy mumbled. "There; let the magic happen."

Benji smiled; he knew something funny would happen because Poppy got the magic words all messed up.

Iggie flew over the house and into Poppy's garage where he kept all kinds of tools and other stuff. Iggie came flying back with a water bucket, a bag full of empty tin cans, an old tennis shoe, and a big chunk of ice.

Grandpa shouted, "Oh, no! This stuff won't work. I don't think Iggie can do magic in Minnesota. Benji, you'd better send Iggie back into the house."

"Poppy, you said the magic words wrong," Benji said, shaking his head. "And that's why Iggie brought you a bunch of junk. Now, say it with me—*uffa huffa muffa wuffa, up, up and away!*"

Poppy got the words right this time, and Iggie flew back into the garage. He came back with an old cap of Poppy's and placed it on the snowman's head. Then he flew away again and returned with two big green buttons. He pushed them with his beak into the snowman's head, giving the snowman eyes. Iggie flew away a few more times and returned with an old carrot for the snowman's nose, an old black piece of cloth that he pecked in for the snowman's smiling mouth, two sticks that he put in Poppy's hands for him to push into the snowman's body for arms. His last trip was for old gloves to go on the ends of the snowman's arms. Then Iggie landed and sat on the snowman's head.

"See, Poppy?" Benji exclaimed. "Iggie did magic, and the snowman is real."

Poppy scratched his head and stepped back to get a good look and fell—*WHOMP!*—into the deep snow.

"Holy catfish, dogfish, sunfish, monster fish," Poppy shouted. "What will people think when they see me sitting in a pile of snow next to an eagle sitting on a snowman's head?"

Benji just smiled. He knew that everyone would like the snowman and laugh over Poppy, stuck in a big pile of snow.

By then it was time to go back into the house... after Benji and Iggie helped Poppy get up from the big pile of snow.

"Tonight let's think up a real good name for our snowman," Benji said.

And that's the story of how Benji and Iggie used magic to help Poppy make a snowman during their winter visit to Minnesota.

Benji and Iggie
Help Santa Claus

As Christmas was getting closer, Benji heard an announcement on the news. Santa Claus had sent out several emails and text messages to let people know he had a big problem. Three of his helper elves were sick with COVID and two of his reindeer also had the virus. With so many out sick, the elves couldn't get all the presents ready for Santa to deliver on Christmas Eve. And he didn't have enough reindeer to pull a sleigh full of presents for kids all over the world. Christmas was super special, and Santa didn't want to disappoint the kids. He was so sad that he cried. Mrs. Claus listened to Santa talk about his big problem, and she thought and thought about how to solve it. Then she had an idea.

"Santa, I remember hearing stories about a young boy named Benji in Washington, D.C. who has a little eagle friend named Iggie. They have done some wonderful magic things for kids. Maybe they could help you this Christmas."

Santa liked the idea. He got out his iPad and began searching to find out more about this boy named Benji and his eagle friend Iggie and the magic they did. He looked in old newspapers he kept about the good things children were doing all year long. He found the story of Benji and Iggie helping firefighters put out a fire and that the fire chief had written a letter to the newspaper about it. He underlined the story of them helping Iggie when he was sick. He chuckled as he read about that birthday party and kids eating cupcakes without using their hands. He knew that Benji and Iggie always used their magic for good and fun things to happen. After lots of searching, Santa was able to talk to Benji on Face-Time and asked if he and Iggie could help him this Christmas. Well, getting a call from Santa himself doesn't happen every day, so Benji was beyond fubblewumped when he saw the name "Santa" come up on FaceTime. Benji could barely believe his eyes when Santa appeared on his screen. Of course, he told Santa, he and Iggie would help in any way they could. But first he had to ask his Mommy, because he would have to fly to the North Pole and be away from home and from her on Christmas Eve. But it turned out his Mommy was very understanding.

"Benji, this will be a wonderful gift you could give to Santa," his Mommy said. "I don't know if anyone brings him gifts for Christmas. And your helping will be a super gift to all the children of the world. Go ahead and help Santa. I won't be lonely. I'll talk with Nanny and Poppy and tell them about how you and Iggie are helping Santa and kids everywhere to have a good Christmas."

Benji worked fast. He waved his magic wand, closed his eyes, and said the magic words, *"Uffa huffa muffa wuffa,* Iggie get here quick." Iggie came flying right into his room in less than a minute. Benji told Iggie how Santa needed super special magic because his helper elves and reindeer were sick with the virus bug. Iggie flapped his wings, hopped up and down, and started flying around Benji's room. Iggie was ready to go, so when he landed Benji knew he should hop onto Iggie's back and get ready to fly to the North Pole. Mommy reminded Benji to put on his winter coat, cap, and mittens because it would be really cold at the North Pole.

Benji closed his eyes, counted to twenty, said the magic words again—*uffa huffa muffa wuffa, up, up and away!* Of course Benji didn't forget to bring his little friends Gwumple, Flossy, Foofie, Crunchy, Pinky, and Don't Forget Grundoon. They could help Santa and the elves too. They started flying high up over the trees, into the sky over New York, over Canada, over the ocean, over Greenland and the frozen North Pole until they landed at Santa's house and workshop. His workshop was big because he needed lots of space for all the presents, and he needed places for the elves to eat and sleep and for the reindeer to live.

Needless to say, Santa was so happy to see Benji, Iggie, and all the little people. He enjoyed talking with Benji about magic.

"Ho ho ho, Benji!" Santa exclaimed. "Your magic is as good as my magic that makes it possible for me to fly everywhere and bring presents to kids." Santa was shouting so loud that he woke up all his helper elves.

"What the hoozy woozy!" the elves said. "What's happening?"

"Hey, elfies, this is Benji and his little friends. They will help us so Christmas isn't ruined for kids. But now we have to figure out how to get all the work done. We only have a few days to get the sleigh ready. I don't have enough healthy reindeer to fly the sleigh. I am fubblewumped and don't know what to do about that."

"Santa, don't worry," Benji said. "Gwumple, Flossy, Foofie, Crunchy, Pinky, and Don't Forget Grundoon will start helping all the healthy elves make toys and wrap presents. Pinky and Gwumple said they would also make hot chocolate. Having a treat like that will help them work extra fast."

The team worked all day and all night. Benji and Iggie loaded all the presents onto the sleigh. But Santa was still worried. Prancer and

Dancer were sick, and the other reindeer couldn't pull the sleigh up into the sky without more help.

"Santa, close your eyes, count to twenty, and say the magic words—*uffa huffa muffa wuffa, up, up and away!*" Benji said. While Santa said the magic words, Iggie jumped into the sleigh harness to replace Dancer and Prancer. Benji and his little friends hopped onto the sleigh with Santa. When Santa opened his eyes he saw all the reindeer, and Iggie right behind Rudolph with his bright red nose, beginning to pull the sleigh up above his workshop, over the fields of snow, and high into the sky.

"On, Vixen! On, Blitzen! On, Rudolph! On, Iggie! Ho ho ho!" Santa shouted. "This will be the best Christmas ever that I bring to kids." And with that, Santa, Iggie, Benji, and all Benji's little friends flew into the sky. They delivered toys and presents to all the kids everywhere.

And that's the story of the Christmas when Benji, Iggie, and their little friends helped Santa.

About the Author

Ben Kohler's playing with words during high school English classes led him into writing poetry throughout his adult years. When his four-year old daughter Julie, during one bedtime demanded a 'real story', Iggie the eagle appeared. Decades later, his grandson, Benji wanted a hundred Iggie stories to fill their FaceTime visits during the long months of the pandemic. Again—Iggie appeared—and the magic began. Grandpa Ben tried hard in his stories—but with limited success—not to get fubblewumped. After writing this book, Benji has become the story teller and Grandpa joyfully his helper with "and then what happened?" Ben lives in Roseville, Minnesota with his spouse, Lorrie.

Praise from a Friend

Several decades ago, Valerie Worth published children's books of what she called Small Poems. At the time I greatly appreciated the way she showed children a way to use language about the ordinary small objects in their lives. I recently had the same response to *Benji and Iggie: The Magic of Friendship*, Ben Kohler's collection of small stories for young children published in Minnesota by Beaver's Pond Press. Kohler celebrates the magical imaginations of young children and the importance of encouraging this imaginative life through the structures of story-making that build on these natural responses.

This unique book... gives support to parents and grandparents and other caregivers who want to create the sense of closeness and warmth that comes with actual storytelling, and who also sometimes just want to read and then let the child retell the story.

I hope that many adults use these tales as starters, in the way the author suggests, and encourage their young listeners to make the stories their own.

Mary Kay Rummel was a regular contributor to *Adventures With Books*, an annual publication of children's book reviews from the College of Education at the University of Minnesota. As a faculty member at the University of MN, Duluth, she taught courses in Children's Literature. She has published nine books of poetry and five books in the field of literacy development and is Poet Laureate emerita of Ventura County, CA.